T0148025

Walking in Fields of Grace

Robert Robinson

authorHOUSE®

AuthorHouse™
1663 Liberty Drive
Bloomington, IN 47403
www.authorhouse.com
Phone: 1-800-839-8640

Published by AuthorHouse 2/28/2012

ISBN: 978-1-4685-0012-7 (e)
ISBN: 978-1-4685-0013-4 (sc)

Library of Congress Control Number: 2011960399

Printed in the United States of America

Table of Contents

A Feathered Bed

There was a pronounced thud followed by a shudder. The shudder sounded more like a muffled groan.

In the morning, we saw the military vehicles—armored trucks and jeeps—shutting off a portion of the highway. Folks around here are used to the Kancamagus Highway being closed during the frost season. But this seemed a little early for frost, just being the first of September—September 5th to be exact. No one would have thought anything about it had it not been for the helicopters. Around here, there's not much chopper activity unless someone is lost and they're conducting a search party.

"What can I get you boys this morning?"

"Eggs sunny side up, bacon, side of toast, coffee."

"Coming right up! You boys kind of closing the highway early! We were expecting maybe three, four weeks of tourists before the road closed."

Silence.

"What happened up there anyway? Some accident?? Anybody get hurt?"

Silence.

"Well, we seen choppers. How many's missing, anyway?"

Silence.

"Guess you boys ain't too friendly. Here's your breakfast. Five dollars each!" He stretched his hand out.

"Hold on, old man. We ain't had time to eat it yet!"

"Oh, you can talk! I thought you was wood, or one of my cows. I mean, Bessie don't talk either. She just chews, if you catch my drift."

"Settle down, old man. We ain't unfriendly. Fact is, I was raised in Littleton, and Jeff here's from Worcester, Tommy's from Barnstead. And Ralph—we don't want to talk about Ralph." He smiled. "He from Cow's End—you know, the non-milking part!"

A quick jab went across the table, landing playfully on Reggie's shoulder.

1

"Now, old man, don't you believe everything this sow's ear is telling you. If anyone knows anything 'bout a cow's end, just ask him about Lucille!"

"Now, you're getting personal, Ralph!" Jeff blurted out. The whole group chuckled.

"What he meant to say was," Ralph continued, "can we get a little more coffee? Please!"

The old man's mood seemed to lighten upon hearing the youthful banter. He was quick to get the coffee, pouring with a half-smile hidden behind a bushy, graying mustache.

"Well, it's just you boys didn't seem too friendly. Around here, people need to know if one of their neighbors is in trouble. Why, we'd all pitch in and help you search. We—"

"Mister, we can't talk much about our mission. We're under orders."

Jeff's eyes seem to plead for the old man to leave well enough alone. His eyes didn't show irritation but frustration. The way his Adam's apple dropped in his throat told that he wanted to talk but just couldn't. The US Army gave him an order, and he just didn't want any trouble.

There was, however, something else that stole from the gleam in Jeff's eyes. Jeff's eyes had sadness in them, sadness too deep for words, sadness that did not come from an army order. He'd seen something and he didn't *want* to talk about it. Any man with a child who's lost a pet has seen that look. It's the stare teenagers give when they want a parent not to ask an embarrassing question.

The old man switched the television to the local news. There was no report of an accident. The soldiers, breakfast half-eaten, slipped out quietly. They did not settle their bills at the cash register, leaving instead their tab and a generous tip on the table. The old man didn't know they were gone until he heard the door shut. Overhead, another trio of helicopters passed. There was something going on.

"Morning, Jed."

"Morning, Everett."

"What do you make of all that noise? Those army boys sure seem quiet. In fact, it's the first time I've ever known the US Army to close the highway. What'd those army boys tell you that were just in here?"

"Everett, I didn't get a wink out of them, excepting the army told them not to talk."

"Well, they're doing that all right. They don't say nothing to nobody. Say, funny thing happened last night. All my clocks, watches, and everything stopped at 10:12. My power came back on, but the Seth Thomas didn't start till I started her by hand. It was about the time of that landslide. "

"Landslide?"

"Yep. Didn't you hear it?"

"Why, yes. I heard something, but I thought it was just my imagination. Sort of like a muffled groan. I thought …"

He paused as if in deep thought.

"Come to think of it, it did sound more like a muffled groan. I just thought it must have been a landslide 'cause I saw all those army boys in town. Well now, Jed, you live more than twenty miles from me, and you heard it too. What do you think it was?"

"Morning, boys."

"Morning, Hollis."

"Jed, I tell you, you're the sorriest cook I ever seen. Can't you keep fresh coffee on the fire?"

"Sorry 'bout that, Hollis. I'll make a pot right now."

"Look here, Jed. You and Everett thinking about re-enlisting? Is that why all those army boys are in town? It's going to take that many to make you old coots get into your uniforms!"

"Hollis," Jed paused, "there's something going on. When's the last time you've seen the Army close the highway?"

Hollis paused.

"Now look, Jed, ain't nothing but some accident. Couple of army trucks run off the road, that's all."

"Then why ain't it on the news?"

"Just watch the six o'clock news. It'll be there. Look, fellows, this is a small town. You don't expect the U S of A Army to blast over all the airwaves about some truck convoy with a flat tire in some little truck stop in Carroll County."

"What about the tourists?"

"I don't want them up here anyway! You don't neither, with their beer cans and their bottles and their paper thrown on the ground. Just send us their money and leave God's green country to God's people!"

"Hollis," Everett interrupted, "did you hear that landslide last night at 10:12?"

"Landslide?" Hollis paused briefly. "Sure, I heard it. 10:12, huh? That's about right. I was watching Humphrey Bogart in *Casablanca* and—"

"It won't no landslide," Everett interrupted.

"It won't?" Hollis replied briskly. "What was it, then?" he asked, peering with intent eyes.

"It was a muffled groan."

"A muffled …" Hollis echoed quickly, then paused, his voice fading away. He had heard it too.

"Hollis, you live twenty miles on one side of the highway, Everett lives twenty miles on the other side of the highway, and I live down here," he said, motioning with his hands, "twenty miles from each of you. I say something happened up there on that highway last night, and no one wants to tell us exactly what. If one of our neighbors got hurt, we ought to know about it. If a couple of army trucks got into an accident, what's all this top-secret hush-hush? Do they really think they're going to drag anything through this town and we ain't going to know about it?"

"Jed."

"What, Everett?"

"It won't no accident. It was a groan, a muffled groan."

Silence fell on the room.

There was no mention of a highway closing on the six o'clock news. No mention of army trucks, bulldozers, or helicopters in Carroll County. No mention of a search party for missing persons. The county sheriff, that bastion of community updates on accidents, stationed himself without any fanfare or communication at a roadblock set up by the army. He didn't even tell his wife what had happened or how long he'd be there. Naturally, townsfolk went out to see what was wrong with the sheriff, fully supplied with choice epithets for his failure to let anybody know what was going on in "their" town. The sheriff's face, however, told it all. It said with deep sadness, "You don't want to know." He looked at his neighbors, and many thought they saw a grown man on the brink of tears. But, they knew that when he said "Git," he meant "git." And he said "git" strong enough and often enough to send out the word: whatever happened was bad. Later on, they'd find out. Later on.

Of course, "bad" and "later on" would never satisfy the old hunters who knew those woods like the backs of their hands. Needless to say, with scopes and rifles in hand, they went the back way at night, ever mindful of the choppers overhead and jittery twelve-pointers in the brush. Hollis did most of the leading, with Jed and Everett in close military formation behind. You don't make much traveling progress with thick underbrush in the dead of night. By 1:00 a.m., the glorious luster of knowing what happened paled considerably from what it had been at the expedition's 10:00 p.m. onset. By 4:00 a.m., three weary husbands past their prime, who had traveled twenty miles of trail for the same effect of three miles as the crow flies, felt the foolishness of not letting the army take care of it. It was 4:13 a.m., and the trio agreed to just climb a few feet farther to the top of the hill before turning around to go home. From the hilltop, they hoped to look through the valley for a possible glimpse of where the action was. At 4:32 a.m., they saw.

He lay in the valley as on a feathered bed, a mile-long form caught between pines on twisting slopes. His albino hair approximated his unsoiled single-piece robe. His hands and feet were in awkward positions, as if losing his balance, he had fallen suddenly, one hand behind his back in a most unnatural posture. His face, for all its peacefulness, could not deny this was a fall, and death had forever sealed his lips.

Now it remained for the army bulldozers to cover this immense form with mounds of dirt. There could be no mistake: this was an extraterrestrial being. No one, *no one*, was looking for UFOs. Everyone who saw him recognized what they saw. It was a place of deep sadness.

In the echoes of their minds, the muffled groan clearly asked a question no one wanted to hear: *if he could fall, what about me?*

The Thump

It was 6:55 p.m. Eastern Standard Time. I'm sure it was not quite seven. *Star Trek* had just gone off. I lay on the sofa wondering whether the Cardassians or Commander Data would solve the mystery. Could the light-year travels of the fictional mind ever materialize in a reasonable form during my lifetime? Of course, the resemblance of real travel apparatuses to Hollywood's fantasies would probably turn out to be far cries apart. But the technological achievement—would it not be astonishing? After all, my generation has seen the birth of the transistor, the PC, optical fibers, the cyclotron, the—

There was a sudden crash. I distinctly heard what I thought was glass breaking, as if someone had taken a rock and broken a window pane. Instead of the noise being out there, the sound seemed close, really close. It was a burglar breaking into my house! I could see the faint silhouette of his scrawny outline, cast by the streetlight shining in my living room window. His left hand moved rapidly, quickly feeling the bits of broken glass. He was reaching for the window lock!

Surely, he must have heard the television. What kind of nut would break into a place knowing a resident had to be nearby? A drug fiend, a desperado, someone who didn't care if he was caught or not caught, someone who didn't care if he suffered bodily harm! Or was he so heavily armed he didn't have to worry? Yes, I thought, it had to be the latter! Physically, he didn't seem imposing enough to be able to rely on brute prowess to subdue the resident. Yes, he had to be armed!

I decided, given my analysis of the thief's weaponry, my safest defense would be to lie perfectly still, as if so sound asleep I heard nothing and knew nothing. Suddenly, he began to pound on the window in rage. He could not locate the opening lever, though his hand seemed to move frantically around it. He muttered loudly in an animal breath that bespoke a rabid lion enraged by hunger. His prey was at hand, and he meant to be fed.

My thoughts pictured worlds of sadistic torture should this fiend gain access. Clearly, the sleep approach might prove naively fatal. Yet, face to face, his weaponry

6

would assuredly prove an overwhelming defeat. I decided escape was my only route of survival.

As quietly as possible, I stretched my right arm across my reclining body toward the door. Rolling over on my stomach, I managed to be a bit shy of touching the knob. With a nervous, tense, semi-panicked stretch, I grasped the doorknob, my right leg on the floor in a kneeling position. As I deliberately turned the knob in a forceful manner, I glanced over my left shoulder for what I expected to be a cautionary glance. To my surprise, he had pulled the lever down. The window was almost open! As the doorknob vigorously resisted my desperate tug, suddenly, his poised form, transfixed in my direction, glared *No escape!*

"Oh, my God!" I screamed. "Oh, my God!"

"Pulse 98, blood pressure stabilizing at 129 over 89, breathing relaxed. ER Mother, do you still want us to inject 40 cc's of—"

"Huh?" I said.

"Mister, can you hear us?"

"Sure, I can," I said.

"You're all right. We're taking you to Broadmeadow General Hospital."

"Broadmeadow General?"

"Yes, sir. You had a heart attack. Nothing to worry about. Just relax. We know what we're doing."

So that's it, I thought. In the bright white light, I saw a mass of tubes. I felt needles in my skin, as if being poked like a pin cushion.

"What happened?" I asked.

"One of your neighbors heard you yelling and saw you on the floor through the half-cracked door."

"And the burglar?"

"The burglar?"

"Yes, the burglar, the *thief*—did they catch him?"

"What?"

"The one who broke my living room window trying to get in? There was glass all over the floor!"

"Mister, we didn't see any glass on the floor. As a matter of fact, your windows don't look broke. Ain't that right, George?"

"That's right," George said as he helped shut the ambulance door. "We'll check it out though."

George was one of two policemen who responded to the 911 call. There was no sign of forced entry, no sign of a crime.

For a moment, I closed my eyes in sheer peace, sensing all was well. Perhaps, I had imagined it all. I didn't much care for needles, but I knew there had to be at least one sedative among those given. So, I could rest, rest, r … e … s … t.

Or so I thought! Curiously, I opened my eyes to stare at three faces intent on doing their jobs. I heard a loud thumping, like the noise made by the thief, or at least the thief I thought I saw. No one in the ambulance noticed.

I heard it again! This time I looked intently at each face. They didn't even acknowledge it. I heard it again, and again, in rapidly decreasing pauses between the thumps. Why didn't they react? Didn't they understand? This was really happening! He was trying to get into the ambulance!

No, No, I thought. "No, no!" I screamed. He was closer than ever before. "For God's sake, somebody stop him!" My last sight: the paramedics scrambling, one with a needle, one pounding on my chest, yelling some obscene language.

It was then I realized that the jump through hyperspace brought some chilling realities I did not anticipate. Listening to my own heart, I had jumped for a split second through hyperspace. In that second, I had released a villain I could not defeat for a battle I had no hope of winning. The thumping of my heart had released me in the darkness of my imagination. There is a time that only a savior can save. Oh that my heart could live forever in the beauty of holiness. It can not live apart from a savior.

Scaling the Ramparts

"The ideal environment of Eden did not prevent the entrance of sin.
A favorable environment is not the answer to man's problems."
William MacDonald, *Believer's Bible Commentary*, Nashville,
Thomas Nelson Publishers, 1995, page 37

The increasing patter of raindrops against the window pulled Chi Wong from his studies. *This new gardener is so strange*, he thought. He had fought his parents' decision to hire one of them, a *tung she*. Why couldn't they hire one of their own? After all, flowers were not new to their culture! And those *tung she*, (*Aagh*, he thought disgustingly), always thought they knew best. No Asian mind could equal theirs, they thought. Now, the "coolie" was the master. The pineapple would make those wannabe Borscht pears stink in the sun.

He sprang from his imperial sofa throne, casting the book aside nonchalantly, as if surprised that its fall from the couch followed the universally acknowledged patterns of gravity.

"What do they know about genetics!"

This house was built by his parents on the fortune saved by his grandfather, who ran the Winged Dragon, the best Schezuan restaurant in Short Pump. Too good for those *tung she*!

Stomping out of the room, his imperial glide unwittingly betrayed his undiminished hauteur. By the early evening light, he could see the gardenias, the roses, the petunias, the begonias, the magnificent magnolias in bloom. Like secreted artist treasure, their smell on any but this moist rainy occasion became an olfactory smorgasbord, an exquisite delirium that only the gods could create in a moment of indulgence—an ecstatic afterthought! To think they let a *tung she* in their garden, a viper so deadly to share the intimacy meant only for them!

"How could they …"

He paused for a moment, suddenly and strangely attracted to the curious motion beneath one of the azalea bushes. At first, he thought it could not be. Yes, it was! Something, someone was digging beneath the bush in the rain.

His eyes grew wide. For one moment, he froze in time, a motionless incongruity on the verge of malice and irreversible disintegration. It was the *tung she* digging in the rain! Did he really think anyone would fall for "that line"? Only a *tung she*, "coolie"!

His thought broke off there. Coolie, he had said, accidentally. Not that this *tung she* did not deserve to be treated as a coolie. But there had to be another word that should be used with a *tung she*. After all, coolie carried some inflections of his own heritage, however faint and demeaning. This *tung she* should not be placed on an equal footing with the struggles of his people. Even if he was on his knees in the rain, no hard labor performed by a soft *tung she* could begin to approach the time-rehearsed, now deified, struggles of his people. Those were the days of unrewarded sacrifices, the makings of myth, the building blocks of cultural history. And no *tung she* was ever worthy of entering that realm, scaling the ramparts!

As he continued his digging, the gardener smiled, as if flooded by some inner contentment. He showed no discomfort at the falling deluge, using its spin off his hands to gently massage kneaded clay and mud around roots of seedlings and off shoots. He seemed as one neither needing respect nor compliments from his patron. It was as if the work alone, his work alone, was overwhelmingly satisfying. With tenderness, his hands established plants in realms of beauty where minds could not shape but only react, transformed, transfixed.

As I watched him fix plant after plant, suddenly his work was through. At the last moment, with a stare that said both "I knew you were there all the time" and "What do you want?" the gardener took a long, haunting look at me before he retired.

"Tung she," I said in a stern but muffled voice. As I turned to return to the sofa, losing my balance on a lump in the rug, I took two frightened, half-stumbling steps before falling, partly catching myself by grabbing some of the books on the dusty shelf. Several of the volumes on that shelf fell, and I was forced to pick them up. Unless, of course, I wanted to hear grandfather's cries/curses! He had always placed such a high value on books, mostly because his "drudge's" life had never afforded him the opportunity to read many books. He collected books almost without thinking, with no real knowledge of their intellectual content. For example, among these fallen books were several used books, novels, that even in their prime probably enjoyed a very slender circulation and even slenderer applause. Here, on the same shelf, besides Mrs. Love-Torn's maudlin romance sat Mr. Pennyworthy's guide to pecuniary prowess in the cultivation of the most banal trinkets. And then there was this big, black leather book, a Bible, "O-o-o-oooh."

"Ha, ha, ha," I laughed, my belly splitting with unrestrained joy, unable to deny the ironies of the moment. My family would never read the Bible, believing only in the spirits of our ancestors. So why keep *tung she*'s book on the shelf? Perhaps Grandfather felt that someday we might have an intelligent conversation with *tung she*, and we could use this book as a starting point. You know, when you get old, your mind is not all there. *I'm sure Grandfather has no idea what's in this book,* I thought.

"Let's see," I said. Surely, there was some passage I could read that could prolong my laughter without disrespecting my grandparents too much for being caught in *tung she*'s stupid web.

"In the beginning was the Word …" *Boy,* I thought, laughing, *these* tung she *sure are bright. How else do you begin a book except with words? Oh, I get it:* tung she *need picture. Poor baby!* Expecting to burst with additional laughter, I read on, "And the Word was God …" *Yes,* I laughed. "And the word was with God …"

"With God?" I said. "With God!" I said again, as if humorously puzzled by the thought of a "Word" being with God. *Not funny enough,* I thought. Flipping a couple of pages, I read:

And I saw heaven opened, and behold a white horse; and He that sat upon him was called Faithful and True, and in righteousness He doth judge and make war. His eyes were a flame of fire, and on His head were many crowns; and He had a name written, that no man knew, but He himself. And He was clothed with a vesture dipped in blood: and His name is called The Word of God. And the armies which were in heaven followed Him upon white horses, clothed in fine linen, white and clean. And out of His mouth goeth a sharp sword, that with it He should smite the nations: and He treadeth the winepress of the fierceness and wrath of Almighty God. And He hath on His vesture and on His thigh a name written, King of Kings, and Lord of Lords. And I saw an angel standing in the sun; and he cried with a loud voice, saying to all the fowls that fly in the midst of heaven, "Come and gather yourselves together unto the supper of the great God; That ye may eat the flesh of kings, and the flesh of captains, and the flesh of mighty men, and the flesh of horse, and of them that sit on them, and the flesh of all men, both free and bond, both small and great."

"O-o-o-oh, scary," I said, laughing all the while. One more passage! I began to read, "Jesus wept." In the midst of laughter, in the middle of a syllable, I came to a screeching halt. My eyes suddenly met the gardener's, *tung she*, standing in the doorway as the rain fell down his body, his face. For one moment, time froze. I slammed the book shut. The gardener moved out of the doorway, out of sight.

For days afterwards, I could not get that picture out of my mind. I kept coming back to that doorway, gasping in that olfactory smorgasbord. Still, it made no sense at all. Until today! Today it is raining again, and through my doorway, our doorway, I see the gardener working in the rain, tenderly kneading his seedlings. He does not look at me, but he knows I am here. And as I thumb through the Bible, I finally happen on that passage I have been pondering for so long. "Jesus wept." "Who is this Jesus?" I ask myself again and again, and the rain does not let up. I read on, and this time I do not laugh. Is it possible that *tung she* can be right? When my eyes meet the gardener's, they are wet with tears. How could I have been so stupid?

> "And when she had thus said, she turned herself back and saw Jesus standing, and knew not that it was Jesus. Jesus saith unto her, "Woman, why weepest thou? Whom seekest thou?" She, supposing him to be the gardener ..." Gospel of John 20:13-15

The Gift

"Do you want to be made well?"
The sick man answered, "Sir, I have no man to put me
into the pool when the water is stirred."
Gospel of John 5:6–7

It was Joseph who noticed first: two large hands slightly waxen, as if the sun had unrestrained blazed on the worker's extremities. He stood motionless for a moment, head down in fixed concentration, a silhouette of twisted sinews and chiseled features. Without a second thought, he reached down and heaved the bundle of shingles upon his left shoulder. Glancing neither to the right nor to the left, he continued his well-rehearsed trek up the ladder, to the roof, and down with the bundle. With nail in hand, he sat down and hammered the shingles in place.

Joe's stare was intense, as if looking for some recognition, some acknowledgment from the face. He wasn't going to school today. His wheelchair and his disease, multiple sclerosis, had infected his attitude to make him a ten-year-old dropout—unofficial dropout, that is. His parents' guilt as drivers of the cars involved in the accident that landed him in the hospital where he got the tainted blood had conditioned them to somewhat regularly let him have his way when it came to school attendance. After all, why make their son go to school where every day he was constantly reminded that he was not normal? Neither parent told Joe or the school administration that their son was a dropout. They merely allowed him to miss school. Unless he crossed one of them, they provided the logical and emotional support for their son to stay at home on any given day.

On this particular morning, Joe wheeled himself out on the porch of their 1950s Victorian mansion.

"Honey! Honey, please! Don't block the door. You know Dad's got to get out in five minutes."

Joe sat transfixed, as if he didn't hear her. Normally, this behavior would have brought a second repetition of his mother's plaintive whine, followed by a stern reprimand. It didn't matter that Joe was blocking the doorway. The whine was for attention. Both father and mother could go around Joe whenever they chose, and by more than one door. But this morning, mother stopped, noticing Joe intently staring at something, or someone (she wasn't quite sure which), across the street.

"Honey …" she paused.

She noticed that the six men working on the Harrison's roof seemed intent about their business. Dressed in cut-off T-shirts and jean shorts, their uniform was so typical of construction workers that she hardly found them worth a second glance. But her son, her son was staring intently. She sensed a discovery had suddenly taken place in his mind amid this rather commonplace scenario.

"Honey," she whined.

This time, it was clear. Her son definitely had not heard a word she said. She turned to get his sister, Margaret, to go to the school bus stop. To her surprise, Margaret was staring too, her eyes locked in a mesmerized circuit going from Joey to the workers to Joey. Margaret, usually talkative and highly sociable for a six-year-old, didn't say a word.

Mother took notice. With one finger pressed against father's lips, she signaled him to remain motionless and watch as their two children were lost in unprecedented silence. Margaret's lunch in hand, mother gently but firmly grasped Margaret's elbow and led her to the bus stop with minimal disruption of Margaret's catatonic observations. Once Margaret was on the bus, Katherine returned briefly to get her purse. The usual good-bye kiss, a peck on the cheek, was executed on Joseph without a spoken word.

"You know, Ward," she said as they pulled out of the driveway, "these children of ours are a strange bunch this morning."

After a brief glance at each other, both parents started a chuckle that did not end for at least ten minutes.

Joe sat on the porch watching the arm movements. He watched what seemed to him artistic excellence as the crew methodically laid the shingles. Occasionally, he would look away at another crewman, but his eyes instinctively were drawn back to the stranger. Joe watched and waited, hoping for the men to strike up some conversation in which he could join. When the conversation began, the other men talked glibly, the stranger said nothing.

Finally, when he could stand it no longer, Joe wheeled himself down the steps. No little task for him, since he had previously learned to balance his weight one tire at a time, one step at a time, until he had trudged all six steps. It was a feat he never let his mother see. He knew she would blow the roof off if she saw her little boy endanger himself. After all, if he fell, there'd be more medical bills to pay, more hospital time to take away work days, more special attention needed to crowd in on an already crowded life. Whenever he had done this in the past, his journey down the stairs seemed like mocking punishment. Today, however, for the same effort, he saw a prize.

Once on the ground, he wheeled right over to the shingles and waited. He knew the stranger would come for a bundle and hoped he would finally say something that would acknowledge Joe. The stranger did get bundles several times but said nothing to Joe. The entire crew could see the fire in the boy's eyes but, the stranger gave no indication that he had noticed that fire. He just walked around Joe, head down.

Finally, Joey blurted, "Don't you ever get tired?"

The stranger paused as if thinking of his response.

"Wish I could carry a bundle like that!"

"Hey, kid, don't get in the way!" a crewman shouted.

With a bundle on his shoulders, the stranger turned as if to go. Joe's heart fell. His face, once beet red with excitement, was now crestfallen leather. He turned his wheelchair and went through the painful step by step up the stairs to the porch. Turning to go into the house, he gave a long look at the stranger and the crew. Inside his house, he left the front door open so that he could look out occasionally if he chose. Most of the day, he spent crying, knowing no one could see him. He thought, *Good little boys don't get hurt!*

There was a knock at the door. A stunned Joe, awakened from an unplanned nap, wheeled to the door. It was the stranger. He was holding a small wooden statue, sturdy, unfinished. The stranger handed it to Joe. It was then that he saw. His eyes met the stranger's eyes for a moment just before the stranger left. Joe watched as he walked down the driveway and got into the back of a waiting pickup truck.

When mother came home that evening, Joe told her about the stranger's gift. He made several observations of the statue from different perspectives throughout the evening. His sister saw it, looked a little puzzled, and went off to play. Whenever she looked at the statue, that same puzzled look returned, as if its configuration was too complex for her young mind to grasp.

"Well," said father, "what are you going to do with that roofer's toy?"

"He wasn't a roofer."

"Oh?" said the dad.

"He was a carpenter."

"And what," a slight laugh in his voice, "are you going to do with that carpenter's toy?"

"It's not a toy."

"Oh! What is it then?"

"It's a gift."

At this point, Ward could barely restrain his laughter.

"Son, a block of wood is a block of wood is a block of wood. You know what I mean."

"Yes, sir," said Joey, despondent. He took his block of wood, went to his room, put it on his windowsill, and went to bed.

In the morning, when he opened his eyes, the sunlight shining on the statue cast a shadow on the wall. Joe, stunned by the statue's shadow, rubbed his eyes a couple of times and then understood. He got up, dressed, walked through the kitchen, kissed his speechless mother on the cheek, and got on the school bus with his sister. His mother and father were late for work that day. The shock of seeing their son walk, a feat they had not seen in over a year, left them in total shock. What in the world had happened? Their son had never said a word.

In Joe's room, the statue on the window sill remained as motionless as it had always been. As the sun moved on its westward course, the shadow on the wall gradually disappeared. Joe's recovery was confirmed by repeated medical tests. The parents, the medical community, and all others who knew of Joe's prior condition were amazed at the reticent child's recovery. Only three people understood how it happened. One, his sister, understood only that the statue had played a part. Joey understood just a little bit more than Margaret. You see, the statue's shadow on the wall was a silhouette of a roofer lifting a bundle of shingles. On the morning he walked, Joey understood that you have to stand up to lift shingles.

It was, however, some twenty years later before Joe understood why there was a hole in the statue the same size as the hole in the carpenter's hand. The exact moment he figured that out, Joe had to kneel. The answer was real simple. No gift is a gift without a cost.

And when they had come to the multitude, a man came to Him,
Kneeling down to Him and saying, "Lord, have mercy on my son,
For he is an epileptic and suffers severely; for he often falls
Into the fire and often into the water. So I brought him to Your disciples,
But they could not cure him." Then Jesus answered and said, "O
Faithless and perverse generation, how long shall I be with you?
How long shall I bear with you? Bring him here to Me." And Jesus
Rebuked the demon, and it came out of him; and the child was cured
From that very hour. Then the disciples came to Jesus privately and said,
"Why could we not cast it out?" So Jesus said to them, "Because of
Your unbelief; for assuredly I say to you, if you have faith as a mustard
Seed, you will say to this mountain, 'Move from here to there,' and it
Will move; and nothing will be impossible for you." (Matthew 17: 14-20)

To Be Avoided

Sorry looks back. Worry looks around. Faith looks up.
—Anonymous

What I am about to say may appear macabre or lacking in taste. It is not intended to be macabre or lacking in taste. Rather, it is a tragedy to be avoided, if possible. Its unusual descriptive setting may suggest embers of irony, sarcasm, fantasy, or insanity. But its basic drift is sincere. Please take it seriously.

Brace yourself: my story begins at my burial. In death, we learn all sorts of things never before imagined. Death itself is just a moment in the continuum, a step where we develop a sixth sense, a guide of absolute certainty as to what is and is not true. No, at death, you don't see stars or fall under the power of incantations from a magical book, or experience some other similar foolish notion. You just know! Maybe it's because the mind is relaxed, not having to bother with bodily functions any longer. Or maybe it's your security in the knowledge that the worst that can happen has happened or will happen shortly. Anyway, it's just an experience. One minute you're conscious, and the next you're conscious. The only difference is no feeling of bodily pain.

Prior to my death, I had always imagined death itself as some frightening experience in which the deceased frantically struggles to retain the power of breath until this insuperable electric shock overcomes. I found that at death I experienced an uncanny ability to see through all objects, except human bodies.

During my burial, I watched as they threw the dirt on my casket. However, at my burial, I had several strange, or shall I say different, experiences that convinced me I had entered a new world. For example, once the dirt covered the casket so that daylight no longer touched it, I lost my ability to see through physical objects. This struck me as quite unusual, as in no time in the past since death had I experienced any difference in sensory abilities. I had seen as well at night as during the day. But suddenly, with a little dirt, I had lost the ability of extraordinary insight.

The next thing that happened at my burial was that my casket disappeared instantly. Within a split second, I found myself with my feet dropping to the floor of some cavern resembling a medium sized, but not large, miner's tunnel. The darkness surrounding me was thick and quiet. Yet, at all times, for some inexplicable reason, I could see my body clothed in its grave garments. Of course, this may strike you as strange, but since death, I had had such a variety of experiences that the strange did not strike me as strange but merely different. In my state of mind, I had come to expect the new and uncertain.

Prior to my death, I had resigned myself to an afterlife, if there were to be such a thing, in a place other than heaven. The residence of perpetual bliss and achievement, heaven, had struck me all my life as the maudlin delusion of stunted minds. Whether one sits on a cloud eternally strumming a harp or fawns in endless stare on a deity, I could not rationally accept an existence I could not control. Before death, I separated the mental from the cosmic, the physical from the moral. My rule in life had always been mind over matter, not the rules of a god over mind or the rules of a demon over mind. Mind over matter, and it was my mind that mattered. The third experience I had at my burial, almost simultaneous with the other two experiences, was an awareness that this was that other place. Quite frankly, I was a little frightened at first, as any person is likely to be in an extremely dark tunnel.

I stood for a while, listening, eyes straining. I saw and heard nothing. I listened intently for some sense of direction but heard not even breathing. I don't know how I was able to do all those things—walk, talk, hear, and not breathe. But as I said earlier, I had come to expect the unusual and accept the different.

There was a still, quiet voice within me that said, "Walk." So, I did. As I said earlier, I could see every part of my body but nothing further, not even the ground on which I stood. I started walking with the small steps any man would take in a dark tunnel without direction, listening for echoes or some sound. I was not unusually afraid.

Suddenly, I saw it, as clear as glass, coming directly toward me, but it moved too quickly to duck. Something flew by me and hit me on the left shoulder. No harm, just a tap. Again, as clear as glass, something else flew by me and inflicted a light tap on the left shoulder. At the speed they were flying, I couldn't make out what they were. I only knew that I didn't like them. I walked on.

For a second, I heard something behind approaching with speed, and then— *wham!* I was flat on my face! Something hit me from behind and kicked me square. It also shoved my head with such force as to make sure it hit the ground. At my fall, I heard voices coming from all directions, hundreds of voices laughing like crazy. I saw no one. I got up, not to be undaunted. It just shoved me and kicked me again. The voices laughed hysterically. This cycle repeated itself a third time, and by the fourth,

I was braced for the obvious. Sure enough, a fourth and a fifth. And then it stopped! And the voices were quiet!

Time six, I figured they were just delaying to make their laughter sweeter. But you know, there never was a sixth time! At first, I stood there waiting for the kick. Then I figured, *Well let's all laugh. I'll walk, and it'll kick.* There was, however, no time six. I walked a little briskly at first and then slowed down. There was only darkness and eerie quiet.

I heard something loud. Funny thing about that cave: you could never tell where the sounds were coming from, like surround sound in stereo. I heard a rumble, real quick like. Then I smelled something. It had to be the foulest smell I ever smelled, a stench so awful every hair on my body stood up. The rumble stopped, and then— voila! I was drenched by an unseen cloud with this foul-smelling water. Equally was I blest with the laughter of my unseen audience. But my thought was terror. I only wanted a shower. This smell was the most repugnant I ever encountered.

I walked a little farther. Ah, again the unseen cloud burst, and the laughter repeated itself. Again, time three. Suddenly, as if materializing from nowhere, I was walking in a field of gladiolas. I had always loved gladiolas for their fragrance. Yet, when I approached to smell them, thinking that their smell might comfort me given my present agitation, so strong was my stench that I could smell nothing but the water. For all intents and purposes, my olfactory nerves were dead. Within seconds, the gladiolas withered in my presence. My pungent aroma was devastating.

Right over my left eye, a big splat of a substance I recognized! My stomach turned. It was thrown in my face! I moved quickly to brush it off, and suddenly, I was bombarded on all sides. As I fought frantically to removes the blotches, a whole army attacked, shoving it down my throat and in my nostrils until my mouth could not move, my nostrils could not smell. I was knocked to the ground, covered with fecal sediment over every inch of my body. When I was finally able to stand, never did I wish a shower more than now. Unable to move my jaws, I was periodically soaked by my little invisible cloud. My new exterior seemed to soak in the water, resulting in my limbs losing almost all of the mobility they had, as the added weight over a period of time made movement nearly impossible. My army of attackers vanished without recognition.

Believe it or not, I managed to still walk, slowly, ever so slowly, like a giant turtle. As I walked, I came to a ditch. In its water, I saw my reflection. I looked like a rock man, square head, detestably lumpy body. I waded across, and while wading, noticed I could hear nothing. At least now I could not hear their laughter.

If this was their way of defeating me, they were mistaken. I would walk as long as I could, until I was immobilized, until I saw him, and only then would I be satisfied. For seeing him would mean the end was near. I didn't care what they did to me. As long as I saw him face to face, saw the cause of my oppression, my misery, I was ready to accept my fate. If anything, these other experiences, objectionable as they were, would be trivial, cake, when I saw him. For he would cast the final blow, and who cares what else he does when you have peace of mind? One of my biggest problems in life was that I couldn't see him coming, and here, how could I avoid his coming? How could he for that matter?

As I walked along, it seemed hours went by at the flip of a hat. The laughing voices now appeared empty beside my anticipation of meeting him. I thought of myself as I was at that moment—taste buds deadened, nostrils deadened, hearing deadened, feelings deadened. Only my eyes and fatigue and curiosity and determination operating. And quiet, so quiet.

A channel. I looked down the channel and saw him in the distance. Yes, it was a light—a light! I raced, but who am I kidding: I trudged onward to the reclining figure in the distance. *This must be! This must be him!*

As I approached, I saw a young man, age approximately twenty-three, dressed in a plaid, blue and black, flannel shirt. He wore jeans, faded jeans, the kind you can buy. His head was propped in his right hand. His skin was smooth. His hair was long. With his left index finger, he was scribbling on the ground. He was slender, not fat, not muscular, not handsome, not ugly. Just regular, I guess. The nearer I drew, the more obvious it became that this was a giant. I thought to myself, *Can this be him, so mild and meek in appearance? Where is the hideous appearance—the clubbed foot, to say the least of the requisite apparel?* In astonishment, I asked over and over again like a dumb mute, *Can this be him?*

I moved in for a closer look. Apparently he was unaffected by my smell. Or was my smell real? Was it still there? He looked to be humming as I approached. Finally, when I stood still for about fifteen minutes, he stopped humming and looked directly at me.

His eyes had the coldness of prejudice. It was a look of friendship that had unmistakable boundaries. Mind you, his look was not one of racial prejudice. For covered as I was from head to toe, I doubt if he could tell if I was blue or purple. His look was one of benevolent condescension. He had, you might say, a look of disrespect. Certainly, you have seen eyes like those before.

So relieved was I, however, to see a human form. I strained to move a jaw or lift a hand, to make some motion of communication. My efforts, as you well guess, were fruitless, immobilized as I had become. Suddenly, I became aware that in this situation mental telepathy had replaced verbal and body language.

He took his index finger and knocked the fecal matter from my left ear.

"Him?" he said in a flat, emotionless tone. "Nobody sees him."

There was a loud peal of laughter. I looked around, discouraged, for my "friends," the voices I heard but did not see. When I looked back, the youth was gone.

I heard one of the voices say, "Let's take him to see Him."

Wonderful, I thought.

"No, no, stupid," referring to me, he said. "Didn't you just hear the guy? Nobody sees him!"

Another burst of laughter.

Another voice cried out, "That is, I mean ... you didn't really expect to see him, did you? But what about Him?"

"Yes!" another voice chimed in. "We'll take him to see Him."

And the chorus of "we'll take him to see Him" grew louder, as if a serious motion at a meeting of intoxicated partygoers.

Him who? I thought.

"Him!" one of them yelled at me. "H-I-M," he spelled it out for me.

I kept thinking *Him who?* until it slipped out.

"You don't mean ..."

There was a loud round of applause and cheering, followed by laughter, louder and louder laughter. I laughed too, thinking they could not be serious. I mean, them taking me to see Him! The minute I started laughing, their laughter died down. The more I thought of it, the louder I laughed, until my sides were aching, tears rushing out of my eyes. Finally, in between a cackle, I happened to open my eyes. I saw them. My laughter stopped quickly but not abruptly. Millions and millions of eyes, filled with spleen and venom, unnerving. For a moment, there was absolute silence. Then suddenly, I realized the gravity of the situation. They were serious, dead serious. Instantly, my tears of joy turned to fire on my cheeks.

"Oh no, don't take me to Him! I need a shower! Come on, now, let's bring this game to a close. I mean, you got me—hook, line, and sinker. What else do you want? I mean, no, no, no, no! Not Him! I don't want Him to see me in this state! Not God! Listen, I need a shower, I need a—"

Splat. All over the left ear. Then a couple of rapid thuds—reinforcements, you might say.

At the thought of seeing Him in my present state, I burned with guilt and shame. So much did I burn that fire engulfed my entire body. I realized that these demons, as in all things in the past, were going to force me against my will to come face to Face, in ultimate shame. The ground beneath my feet began to quiver (I pleaded) and gave a mighty surge toward the light, a small pinhole in the ceiling. The closer I got, the more I burned. The last thing I remember before I went insane was rapidly approaching that pinhole, burning hotter, begging in urgent desperation, "Please, please, don't take me to see Him! Not Him!"

Friend, if you can, please avoid my fate. There is no truth where I am, only deception. There is no will. There is no hope. There is no moral consciousness. Please avoid this place.

And if you must come and join the other voices, please don't take me to see Him. Please!

> For by grace are you saved. It is the gift of God, lest any man should boast. Ephesians 2:8

> For we must all appear before the judgment seat of Christ; that every one may receive the things done in his body, according to that he hath done, whether it be good or bad. Knowing therefore the terror of the Lord, we persuade men; but we are made manifest unto God; and I trust also are made manifest in your consciences. 2 Corinthians 5:10-11

A Familiar Face

For now we see through a glass, darkly,
but then face to face.
1 Corinthians 13:12

"Excuse me," he said, shuddering, as if overtaken by embarrassment. His eyes fell upon the fellow traveler with a look of protracted agony.

"I was wondering if … You so much resemble him; your face is so familiar …"

His voice drifted off in that moment of a monologue that had been intended to begin a dialogue. Though physically present at an airport gate at Boston's Logan Airport, his mind traveled forty years and six thousand miles in a split second to a battlefield both blurred and clear. Clear: he remembered the sickening colors, the rancid hot sulfuric stench of burning ammunition, the sounds of endless exploding ordinance, the scamper along the ground of a trail of bullets that ran after him as a rabid dog. He ran with every ounce of energy that he could muster to escape the remorseless finger of death lodged in the canine's tooth. In a hail of bullets that seemed to come from every direction simultaneously, he dove into a foxhole, the only shelter in sight. As he dove, his surroundings outside of the foxhole became a blind spot—a blur that the conscious mind records but only the subconscious mind sees in a landscape of dreams, distorted emotions, and supersonically articulated prayers.

In the hole, within a moment, he sensed a presence he had not imagined during the dive. There was someone else in the foxhole with him, someone who evidently jumped in the same time that he dove. For once his feet touched the bottom of the hole, he remembered another's body part, perhaps an arm or a leg, that grazed his body during the descent. Now every good soldier knows that in combat instinct kicks in to save a man's life when the deliberations of a conscious mind would lead to a fatal conclusion. In other words, when jumping into a foxhole, a man's subconscious not only informs of any danger in the hole in a single glance but also guides him to abort a dive and seek another hole if the danger is beyond that which the soldier can handle.

23

To have dove into that hole and encountered another body meant that that body was not there during the glance. Such a body had to be part of the landscape of the blur, something visible but not seen while fleeing the determined rabid canine.

Turning quickly, he expected to see the insignia of a fellow comrade at arms. But this encounter had the mark of an unscripted nightmare! For when he turned, he saw a mirror: a man of the same height, same build, same fear as himself. Only this man's insignia bore the unmistakable identification of the enemy! For a moment, he froze, his pounding heart drowning out all surrounding explosions. He would have shot the enemy, but he was out of bullets. He had lost his bayonet somewhere as he ducked and dodged to save his life. He sat, alas, with no usable weapon but his fist, looking at a twenty-year-old male in good health with a rifle.

As the bullets overhead grazed the foxhole's lips, causing him to involuntarily lower his head and torso, he sat for a moment in a limbo world, between instant death outside the hole and delaying death inside the hole. Even the motion of ducking to save his life from the stream of bullets overhead seemed useless as he considered his enemy was in the same hole sharing his breath, his body odor. And this enemy in the hole was one from which he could not conceal his fear!

It was only a moment that he sat motionless. To him, that moment seemed a cold sweat eternity. This snapshot of helplessness and despair was broken when he realized the enemy in the hole had not shot him or stabbed him. In fact, the enemy made no immediate motion toward him whatsoever. At this close range, looking directly into the enemy's eyes, he saw the same fear he had. While he waited for a gunshot, thinking first, *Any minute now*, and then, *What can I do?*, the silence in the foxhole unleashed a stream of memories he could not control or deny. In that moment, he thought of relatives, friends, and a sweetheart, all far away in a battle-free existence. He recalled scattered highlights of his life and questioned why in the corona of those highlights the end should be now and in this way.

But that subconscious mind—it kicks in to tell you something's wrong with this picture, something's out of kilter with the facts of the moment. Consistently ducking, involuntarily, the stream of bullets that seemed to be edging their way down the sides of the foxhole to a restrained limit, the subconscious mind reveals the truth. The enemy in the hole had no bullets either. Nor did he have a decisive weapon he could use to save his life.

The so called "foxhole" was not a foxhole either. Rather, it was a crater, a hole in the ground dug by previously fired gun shells. That these two combatants used it as a foxhole was commendable but shortsighted. The pockmarks of battle are not designed with the maneuverability expected in a foxhole. In other words, hand-to-hand combat, however noble and within the wishes of the high command, was not an option. This foxhole boasted two disoriented victims who were pinned down in a carnage scene where the only option for survival at that moment consisted of remaining motionless until the gunfire died down. At such a time as the hole occupants found themselves, inflexible notions of heroism, bravery, and treason had to be discarded. One's visualization of who the enemy is blurs as helplessness and unmistakable immediate threat can neither be denied nor defeated by the weapons at hand.

"Sir, I'm sorry," he said as he looked into the traveler's eyes. "It's just …"

His mind recalled how he had been rescued from that hole. After what seemed like hours, maybe it was minutes, maybe it was a half a day, a face suddenly peered over the side of the foxhole and pointed directions. It was clear by the pointer's hand signals that he meant *get out of the hole and run to safer ground*. It was also clear that he pointed in opposite directions at the same time. Somehow, his eye contact gave each man the sense of direction he was to take when escaping the hole. In a split second, each occupant leaped from the hole and ran in the indicated direction. One must not think this run was a peaceful jog to waiting arms of exuberant comrades. Rather, the run proved a desperate, all-out exertion, a gun leg between bullets and obstacles. He ran as hard as he could, without a rifle, or any other weapon, from the shelter of a tree to an overturned truck to a wall behind friendly lines. Later that evening, he met other grunts from his side who shared a weapon and ammo. And the war went on.

"It's just," he continued, "I've spent all my life looking for one man—a pointer, really. He saved my life some time ago during the war. I know he's dead, but you know, one hopes against hope. I mean, he couldn't have survived with his arms stretched out like that amid all that gunfire! But somehow … your face—it looks so much like his. I apologize, and I hope you will pardon an old man's folly. Was …" he hesitated for a moment, nervous, "was your father ever a pointer in the war?"

"For the Jews require a sign and the Greeks seek after wisdom:
But we preach Christ crucified,
Unto the Jews a stumbling block and unto the Greeks foolishness."

1Corinthians 1:22-23

Second Chances

Lucy's eyes sparkled as she curiously viewed the stranger. He did not fit the mold of a shiftless migrant with hardened cheekbones and the unkempt demeanor of the other hands. This one was different. She struggled with his unusual presence and her assured assessment of other hired hands. For her, proper classification meant you knew how to act around this one for safety and results. How odd, she thought. His silence was so telling.

"What are you doing?" said Jake. "Don't tell me you've got this one all figured out too!"

Lucy nodded up and down a few times, affirming her keen judgment.

"No child of six could possibly be as accurate as you are!" Jake retorted.

"I am not a child, Jake Manners. I am a growing young lady."

"Young lady?"

"That's right. If you don't believe me, ask Nana," she said, referring to Mrs. Edith Johnson.

"Ah, come on! You don't believe everything adults say?" Jake said with a biting cynicism and smugness in his voice.

"Listen, Mister," Lucy darted back, "just because I'm good doesn't mean I'm not a growing young lady," she said, referring of course to her previous accuracy with the hired hands. "Betcha he stays less than a week!"

"A week! Aw, come on, Lucy, give the guy a break!"

Jake's voice reached a convincingly shrill, high pitch. As they argued over the tenure of the hired help, the Nebraska sun descended behind a thicket of grey cumulus. It had been a hot day. Most of the hired help hated the Kansas Surges, those days of hundred-degree-plus heat that made work unbearable, to put it mildly. Still, the hay needed bailing if the cows were to eat that winter. It had been twenty-one straight days of Kansas Surges, with no relief in sight. Most farm hands quit rather than work for minimum wage in such heat. But this one was different!

So involved were the ten- and six-years-olds in bickering that they did not hear the dinner call, though mother plainly sounded the triangle to call all hands. Mrs. Manners had thought the tradition of the triangle added a historical touch that distinguished their family's continuity. Of course, other farms used electric horns and even cell phones on occasion. But Mrs. Manners doggedly clung to what she viewed the definition of distinction: tradition!

The darkening canopy of clouds above seemed an apparition that brought neither rain nor cooler temperature. Such useless celestial phenomena might occasion an artistic sunset, but this was a farm, not an art colony! The sun was expected to set every day, just like the worker was expected to work every day. Reliable help, however, was hard to find, particularly under these conditions. And you dare not pay more than minimum wage! For as surely as you offered and paid more, the help quit sooner, preferring to live off the dollar in hand rather than toil in the field.

"Lucy, Jake! Let's go! Wash for dinner."

As they went inside, extremely scant notice was given to the shifting clouds. The hired help ate separately in an adjunct to the barn. They had their own cook and a meal generally consisting of meat and low-cost staples. A farmer that fed too well lost. At least, that's the way the Manners saw it. "Lazy ignorants," Mr. Manners called them. "A batch of drunks, the whole lot of them!"

"Adam, what are you doing?"

"Mom, will you witness something? I bet Jake a banana that the new man stays less than a week."

"What?" said mother.

"I just want him to pay up *this time* when he loses!"

"Lucy, you know you're not supposed to gamble."

"There, blabber mouth! Next time, you'll learn to wait your turn."

A sudden gust of wind.

"Her turn at what?" mother enquired.

"Mom, I've told her a million times: children should be seen and not heard."

"Jake Manners, I am not a child. I am—"

A sudden gust of wind.

"That's enough, you two! Lucy, you are a child. Jake, you're a child also. You're both my children, and I don't want to hear any more of this silly wagering about who stays and who goes. And no, Lucy, you cannot have Jake's lunch," meaning the banana in Jake's lunch box left from his trip with Nana to the science museum that morning.

"Adam?" Where was that boy?

"William?"

"Coming, Martha."

Since Adam's return from school, the Manners' household had been in a stir. Not only was he nine years older than Jake, which to his parents seemed an eternity, he was an accomplished college freshman whose non-adolescent ideas presented a formidable, even unnerving, challenge to a vision of tradition well-meant but questionable. Supper with Adam meant a few comments, mostly innocent, that assailed the stifling walls of their secure domestic bastion as if Atilla the Hun was arriving with Ghengis Khan in tow. To be honest, the Manners felt his challenges a sudden gust of wind, welcomed because they were needed and whose source was known. Or so they thought! Dinner with Adam was a meal they looked forward to.

"Adam?"

She turned her head and saw this figure slipping quietly into a chair at the table. He gestured for the younger two to take their seats. With a stern gaze and a firm but moderately toned voice that trailed off to quietness, he warned them, "You can't believe everything adults say."

"What?" said mother. "What's that about adults?"

"I learned that from Kierkegaard."

Mrs. Manners drew a totally blank stare. "Kier … Kier …"

"Well," Adam continued as Mr. Manners took his seat, "Professor Cuppett, my religion professor, pointed to the dangers of relying on others."

Now both parents and both children looked at Adam with blank stares.

Mrs. Manners started, "So …"

"So," Adam picked up, "Lucy shouldn't take Nana's compliment too seriously, too literally."

"Oh," said Mrs. Manners, whose paused response reflected the relief of the group. She added, "Neither I nor Bill took a course in religion in our days. Did we, Bill?"

"No, that's right," he said as he grabbed a roll and passed the basket to a waiting set of hands. "When it came to religion, your mother and I boned up on R&R."

"You mean they didn't have computers in your day, Dad?"

"No, Lucy. Dad's from the old school. In his day, they had writing and arithmetic. He and Mom didn't like reading. Right, Dad?"

"Not quite, son," he said to Jake. "When we grew up, church was the place people played—I mean talked—about religion."

His lame pun did not sit well with Mrs. Manners, despite his smile and her understanding of his obvious effort to make light his comments. She saw the drop in the little ones' eyes when the word church was mentioned. The Manners were not a churchgoing family, all previous attendances having been unanimously deemed boring and irrelevant by all family attendees. And, as for God—

"How'd we get on this subject anyway?"

"Well, honey," said Mother, looking at Adam, "I don't think encouraging your brother and sister to question adults is the proper take on your professor's comments."

"Honestly, Mom! Mr. Cuppett was quite strong on that point. He said adults tell children lies every day, and that's why morals are eroding so sharply."

"Lies?" she repeated, her voice ascending toward a fever pitch.

"Lies," he said, "such as, there is a God, or a hell, or an angel, or the Bible is true, or … I mean, you get the picture."

"Well, honey, they aren't lies. They're just—"

"Well, you don't believe them, right?" Pause.

"Well, we believe some of them."

"Like what?" This time Adam looked from parent to parent with a blank stare.

A sudden gust of wind, this one longer and louder than the rest.

Pausing for a moment, turning for support, she looked to Bill, whose anguished grimace made it clear that talk about religion was through today at this table. After all, he didn't have an answer and even for the sake of his child did not want to address any misgivings, any breaks in understanding he or the other family members had. As far as he was concerned, religion, God, was taboo and too big for his mind. His job, Martha's job, was to raise the family, taking care of them the best they knew how with all their hearts. God was fine for raising crops, taking care of the weather, old folks. When He moved into the house, He was not welcome. But now he didn't want to say that before the children! I mean, God was sort of kin to Santa Claus. No good parent takes Santa from his kid!

"You know, we might make a few dollars this year if we could get the help to stay on the job. I swear, you have to watch them at every turn. Why, this one guy insisted on putting a truckload of hay bales smack dab in front of the lawnmower shed, the fool. I swear—lazy ignorants!"

"See, I told you! And it was the new guy—wasn't it, Dad?" Lucy inquired.

"How'd you know that?" said Dad.

"Okay, Jake, you get to do pots and pans tonight!"

"No way! You're just bluffing. Dad didn't say it was the new guy."

"Yes, he did. Didn't you, Dad?"

"Yes, it was him …" Bill paused, and then continued, "The way he stacked those bales, you'd swear he was expecting the cows to come up and do self-serve from the pile. I tell you—"

Another gust of wind, this one louder, more violent than the rest. By chance, Martha peered through the kitchen window. The sky had become ominously dark. She thought she saw a …

"Bill," she said in a loud, declarative tone, "take a look at this. I thought I saw …"

Bill moved the curtain aside to get a better view. Just off in the distance, you could faintly see a little funnel begin to grow. As they stood there in rapt attention, suddenly Bill knew he had to sound the twister siren. Quickly barking orders to the kids, he ran to the shelter, all the while lamenting, *Another year's crop lost to drought and storm.* Why couldn't he win? His cattle would starve to death. The wheat would be uprooted. The corn was already at the point of no return. One more disaster, and they may as well sell the place—or, better still, give it to the bank lock, stock, and barrel. As he raced to the shelter, mumbling curses under his breath, he was surprised to see the new hired hand holding open the shelter door, beckoning the family to enter.

"Well, aren't you a cutie!" Adam said. "You do valet parking too?"

For some reason, none of the other hands made it to the shelter before the door had to be closed. Perhaps, Bill thought, they took refuge in some part of the barn. Bad idea, but what do you expect from lazy ignorants?

The shelter door was locked with only the family and the new hired hand inside. As the storm crept past, the frightening wind—the exploding booms—reverberated in the ears of all. Lucy thought she heard cows mooing in the wind, but she was afraid to say a word. The sound of a thousand freight trains was so loud and so close, fear gripped the family as they expected the shelter door to be ripped off in an eye blink. Grasping the handle, the new hand held the door in what seemed an iron grip until the outside noises hushed.

"My," said Bill, staring, shaking, and helpless, "never seen that before." His voice trailed off, overcome with fear as he witnessed the farm hand holding steady the wooden door and imagined the strength needed to perform such a feat in such a storm.

Emerging from the shelter, Bill found that the hay bales stacked by the hired man against the tool shed had been redistributed by the wind to form a wall at an acute angle to the shed. Behind that wall, nine field hands, having been too disoriented to find the shelter door, lay crouched, safe but shaking.

"Well," said Bill, "we got through this one. No one was hurt, just everything was lost!" He was, of course, referring to the yet uncalculated crop loss, cattle loss, equipment loss, total demolition of their brick ranch house, and the total demolition of the recently renovated barns. All of their vehicles were smashed, either upside down or sitting on their sides at fascinating angles. Amazingly, only the tool shed was not touched.

"I just can't seem to get ahead. Why doesn't God just take it all?"

At that moment, turning as if on cue, Lucy gave the stranger the oddest look. She nudged Jake, who looked just as swiftly and curiously. The stranger did not appear shaken or in any manner to have changed his demeanor. For a moment, Lucy and Jake thought they saw something in the stranger's eye.

"Why doesn't God take it all?" Bill ranted.

"He did, honey," Martha chimed in despairing sarcasm. "He did!"

"What do you think, Mister?" Lucy asked, addressing the stranger. "Did God take it all?"

The stranger looked at Lucy, then Jake, then Adam, then Martha, then Bill, as if by eye contact communicating a moment of introspective meditation focused on each individual. When he looked back at Lucy, who was expecting an oral response, she was astonished to see sadness written on his face. He picked up his shirt and walked away.

Lucy won her bet, but the family was not the same. As the stranger walked down the road away from the epicenter of the cataclysm, every eye fixed on his back in anxious silence. Both family members and hired hands recognized that they owed their safety from the storm to the departing stranger. However, neither the family nor the hands were able to overcome their immediate circumstances and thank the man whose name no one bothered to ask. It was as if his departure revealed the gravity of the situation, exposing their vulnerabilities and helplessness.

The next day, the neighbors showed up and put the family up while Bill and Martha began picking up the pieces. All was not lost, as the insurances kicked in to jump start the farm again.

Adam's computer was lost though, never to be seen again. He was ready to be "over" this tragic experience until a portable radio loaned to him by one of the neighbors accidentally fell while Adam was shaving. Already on, the fallen radio shifted its channel and its volume as a result of the fall. It was then that Adam heard the bars of the song that shook his world and brought him face to face with reality, with himself. For before he could take any action to retrieve the fallen radio, it blared:

> Well, who is this angry man I see
> In the mirror looking back at me?
> It's a man who's tired, a man who's weak,
> And it's a man who needs a Savior.
>
> And who is this fearful little child
> Crying out for home, lost in the wild?
> With a lonely heart that's fading fast,
> It's a child who needs a Savior,
> A child who needs a Savior
>
> And what is this longing in my soul
> That I get so scared and angry?

I need more than just a little help.
I need someone who will save me:
Come and save me!
I need someone to save me.
Who will save me?
Come and save me.

And who is this one nailed to a cross
Who would rather die than leave us lost?
He's come to rescue us, come to set us free.
Hallelujah, hallelujah!
It is Christ the Lord, Our Savior.

Frozen, deathly still, Adam's eyes let drop a tear, then two tears, then a small rivulet. He would have kept crying, but he felt a weight on his shoulder. Turning, he expected to see his father, or some other male, in this private moment in his boudoir. He saw no one, but the weight on his shoulder felt so much like what he imagined the stranger's hand to be like. At that moment, Adam knew the truth and could not deny it. His family had been given a second chance to get it right, from the dignity due to the hired hands to the definition of those life values that really mattered. God had only taken enough to get their attention.

If our message is obscure to anyone, it's not because we're holding back in any way. No, it's because these other people are looking or going the wrong way and refuse to give it serious attention. The devil who rules this world has blinded the minds of those who do not believe. They think he can give them what they want, and they won't have to bother believing a Truth they can't see. 2Corinthians 4:3-4

Remember, our message is not about ourselves; we're proclaiming Jesus Christ, the Master. 2Corinthians 4:6

Grateful acknowledgment is made to Sparrow Song for permission to reprint the lyrics from "Savior" by Steven Curtis Chapman, © 2001 by Steven Curtis Chapman.

The Rush

I will give you the treasures of darkness, riches stored in secret places.

Isaiah 45:3

It seems so odd. Each morning I awake in a strange place. This morning, Gertrude threw a little water on my face. It had doubtless been sitting beside some fireplace. For normally water in wooden buckets did not feel so warm, so comfortable. "Where am I, my God?" I ask. This Gertrude creature, this is the first time I laid eyes on her. In fact, this is the first time I laid eyes on any of the surrounding creatures, the citizen patrons of this place. I keep asking that same question—"Where am I, my God?"— morning after morning, with barely a change in my inflection. You see, each morning, I have an almost identical waking experience. Sometimes it's in a tavern, sometimes an inn. Sometimes it's in a person's home. I wake not knowing where I am or how I got there.

You see, this land is a rush. The citizens appear to have jobs. One is an innkeeper, another a farmer. Several seem to be tradesmen. There is always an aristocrat present, one with superior mercantile gifts and talents. There is at least one braggart in the crowd and one self-styled philosopher. And always one who takes me under his wing!

"Come along now, Thomas," he says to me. Of course, my name isn't Thomas, but I know to whom he is referring. "We must be in Silverville by sunset." Silverville— that's always the other town.

As I step into the light, I am fascinated by the architecture. The town in which I stand always looks the same as the other towns and yet is peculiarly different. I must confess, I have never seen towers that twist as these or roofs with tiles so ornate in their glazed coloring. Some mornings, the road on which we walk is paved, and some mornings just plain dirt. There never is a sign I recognize on any of the buildings, and yet, they're all so familiar.

"Now, Thomas, keep up," he jibs lightheartedly.

The citizenry seem to go about their businesses, both male and female. Occasionally, there are children with the families. I follow close on his tracks, almost bumping into him as he stops to examine the displays in a window or pauses to facilitate traffic along the path. I have no idea where we are going—that is, the exact location in the town to which we travel.

At some time during the course of the day, I will notice a fellow traveler going in the same direction and begin a conversation. After thoroughly enjoyed dialogue, that traveler will break away, at an oblique, off to his destination. Soon, another traveler, or a group of travelers, fills the road space of my last conversant, and the conversation begins anew on the topic the last traveler ended.

After some time, we arrive at an inn and stop to have a meal. I have no money that I know of, but the host feeds and dines me anyway. You must not think me a glutton or sot! I never indulge in gluttony or drink to the point of passing out. I usually have perfect control of body and mind until the meal has long ended and the dishes cleared.

And then the rush occurs! A frenzy overcomes the citizenry, and no one dares to be on the street after sunset. I have often asked if there is some evil that emerges at sunset. Is there some disease, some catastrophe, some urgency in the sunless sky that a man should fear to journey? Sometimes a blank stare from a nearby patron will indicate my question was heard, but a serious reply by any patron will not be forthcoming.

The night usually ends the same. I am enjoying the conversation of several patrons, so much so that I want us to never part. I fall asleep at the table or on a bed provided by my host. When morning arrives, I never again see the patrons I enjoyed the night before. Indeed, when I inquire of their whereabouts, no one acknowledges knowing or even seeing the patrons to whom I refer.

And the building in which I awake, it looks so different! I could swear that overnight the shapes of the tables changed, and the wall coverings are different from those of the previous night. Even the face and dress of my traveling companion is different from that which I recall. All seem bent on conducting daily business in their characteristic manners. The air of fear that pervaded at sunset is no longer present.

Tonight, however, I have determined to spend the night outside. I want to see what monster, if any, this darkness contains. I am convinced this frenzy is foolishness, the fancy of jaded minds in self-absorbed titillation. For I have never seen evidence that some peril decimated a traveler or his entourage in the night! I have never met anyone who was out even a portion of the night! I have concluded this frenzy is delirium, the opiate of the masses frightened by their own shadows.

As the day waxes later and later, I position myself near a backdoor, so that neither my host nor the night's patrons will notice my departure. As I notice various patrons yawn, I feign equal fatigue and convey that horizontal inclination is the remedy to placate my mental dissolution. Laying my head on the table with my eyes shut for several minutes, I reinforce the perception of fatigue. Finally, at a moment when I sense the attention of the alert patrons is focused on others, I slip through the backdoor without fanfare or anyone calling out that I have gone the wrong way.

Outside in the dark, I notice that it is quiet and unimaginably still. The night has a calm that seems serene and disarming. This night is a moonless fresco, an overwhelming pause between movements in a dramatic symphony, exciting and unforgettable. How did fear become attached to something so utterly impotent? Is there truly some malevolent creature lurking that the night should be so universally shunned? This frenzy, is it not the fruit of an old wives' tale, a cowardly failure that hides the truth?

As I ruminated on past cultural responses to this part of nature I deemed vilified and not appreciated, I sat in a corner of the back porch, innocently gazing into the uniform darkness. I yawned as I boringly contemplated the teachings of so many sermons and lectures against my current behavior, all unsolicited and supposedly with my good in mind. Yet, here I sat enjoying a panorama, with no other human to share this experience. In the morning, I would announce to all that I stayed out all night and no evil befell me.

I suddenly felt the lick of a large tongue on the right side of my face. Evidently, while meditating on the world's shortfall, I had fallen asleep. For the tongue that licked me had come from a creature so near I could feel the heat of his breath. Yet, I did not notice the creature's approach.

He stood motionless, silent, faintly visible in the darkness. His leonine red eyes glared with hatred that intensified as the observation timeframe lengthened. I was paralyzed with fear. A creature stood before me in the final moment before attacking! I had no weapon of defense! I had not provoked him! My heart beat feverishly, each thump louder and louder, so much so that I became a sound more than anything else—a sound of foolish arrogance faced with an unyielding menace, isolated and terrified. As he moved to pounce, my whole being melted in the realization that there would be no tomorrow for me. The stench of his breath betrayed a history of feral, merciless assaults.

"There you are," my host said. "Come now, we must be going."

Instantly, I raise my head from the table and stare in disbelief at the sunlight streaming through the windows. I am in the same inn at the same back table as the night before. Could this be possible? Was what I saw only a dream? How is it that the creature did not destroy me?

"Now, Thomas," he pauses. "Still doubting?"

Suddenly, I realize that it was *his* arm that yanked me from the unrelenting jaw of the predator. Yes, yes, yes, it was *his* hand I felt! For I remember its grip, so firm and commanding, so tender and comforting. *How did he know* where I was? Why did he risk himself to help me? As I look into his eyes, I see compassion, such compassion—only possible from one who walks with you, intimate in pathos, resilient in hope.

"Now, Thomas," he pauses. "Still doubting?"

As he asks, he gently lays his hand on my shoulder. I nod, indicating the doubt gone. I rise instinctively to follow, much more so than I have done in the past. But now I understand the rush.

Did I find a treasure in darkness? Yes, *his* hand. That, friend, is enough for me.

Jesus answered, "Are there not twelve hours in the day? If any man walks in the day, he stumbleth not, because he seeth the Light of this world. But if a man walks in the night, he stumbleth, because there is no light in him." These things said He: and after that, He saith unto them, "Our friend Lazarus sleepeth; but I go that I may awake him out of sleep." **John 11: 9-11**

An Uncommon Mercy

"Yes, I know! I was there!" I said, wiping my brow. "I remember each detail." The blazing sun heated the tiled road above the temperature that blistered bare feet. The tombstones and wild grasses were to be expected. Yet little comfort could be found in the green of the grass or the design of the stones. For this was lonely ground whose caretakers, Pain and Oblivion, parched the memory and incompleted aspirations of the tenants.

"My father's father and my father's father's father are buried here. Of course, they are not alone," I said, referring with a decelerating wave of the hand to the rows of others entombed there.

Reflecting, I could hardly forget "that" moment. I had been so absorbed in his assault. Running up, I had grabbed him with all my power, a death lock upon a relaxed, virile, focused itinerant. Thinking to tear the flesh off his back, a continuum of flashbacks exploded before my eyes in intense, horrifying fury. I saw assaults on other travelers, heard screams and cries melting in a reverberating sea of pitiless violence. I saw flashbacks in which falling streams of blood always multiplied, some streams trickling to the left and some trickling to the right. Some fell from foreheads while others gushed from arms and necks. Robes were stained with bloody blotches as dusty feet moving with ever increasing violence departed in full flight, dodging, veering, leaping as they flew. These flashbacks had been my life, played over and over again in razor-sharp kaleidoscopes as I struggled with each passerby. The more desperately the passerby struggled, the more intense and violently was aroused the urge to maim, to hurt, to conquer.

Locked in the itinerant's arms, a stranger, I had had only one question. I had been the wealthiest man, a man who never had to go to Jerusalem or any other center of commerce. They came to me! From my garden kiosk, I commanded the silver that fed Caesar's army, the gold that decided which nations lived and which died. My gestures and emotions became the pulse of creativity, or the sword of destruction, as far as the eye could see. Men didn't dare speak my name for fear an imperfect inflection would bring death's breath from a host of toadies ever desirous of my favor. My frown was dreaded. My grimace assured annihilation. Such had been my life before this graveyard.

"Why?" my eyes cried out, looking at the stranger's.

The world's center of power had shifted since the onset of my dementia. In the graveyard among the silent dead, my despotic accomplishments rotted with a malevolence that exceeded the decay and oblivion that engulfed the loved ones entombed here. Though others had tried to restrain me, so fervent and unrelenting was my dementia that the chains broke regularly, flimsy reminders of the time I chained the world. In my lunacy, the living were all too willing to abandon me to the acres where the bodies found could not ameliorate my suffering.

But then this stranger came! Fresh from prayer, he held me with the compassion beyond that of a loving brother. In the stranger's arms, I regained a composure not known for years. Why? Why did he do that? Why did he not leave me like all the rest—a miserable, putrid smelling wretch who had nothing to offer? What did God see in me that He performed two miracles at once, healing a wounded body and simultaneously enabling a healthy mind to replace the demon-filled refuse that resided there for so long?

"So, you, Judas, you think you can find peace here, among the dead? I told you I was there! I saw them nail his hands and his feet to that cross! Do you really think this one that rescued me from this graveyard is Himself coming here to stay? No matter what lies were told to poison the soul, I know what I saw."

> Hereby perceive we the love of God, because He laid down His life for us: and we ought to lay down our lives for the brethren. But whoso hath this world's good, and seeth his brother have need, and shutteth up his bowels of compassion from him, how dwelleth the love of God in him? 1 John 3:16-17

The Promise

When thou passest through the waters, I will be with thee …
Isaiah 43:2

"Baby, it's all right." She sought to comfort us.

"Baby, it's all right," she repeated, her voice bathed in dulcet sadness. Her eyes searched my face and Irene's face in the expectation of agreement with the marvelous determination she pronounced. We were the family she was leaving behind, the only offspring of her children that had not been killed when the tractor trailer plowed into the bus. They had chartered a bus to pick up family members en route to the family reunion. We were supposed to be on that bus, but the bus never made it to our stop. Our parents were on the bus acting as guides to show the bus driver the way. The bus had stopped at the traffic light at 3rd and Main when the truck slammed into the bus in the rear, causing the bus to go over the side of the bridge and into the river. I guess it didn't matter who could swim and who couldn't. The policeman said they never had a chance, the river being in flood stage. They think the driver fell asleep. There were no skid marks on the bridge. Anyway, how does a driver fall asleep at 11:00 in the morning? It just didn't make any sense.

"Baby?" She paused, waiting for me to say something.

"Yes, Grandma."

"Baby, you stay close to Irene."

Irene was my nine-year-old sister.

"Don't let them separate you. I had a talk with the Lord, and He assured me it was going to be just fine."

She wouldn't have been in this hospital bed if it wasn't for me and Irene. With the folks all dead, we stayed with Grandma, as she was all we had left. She only had her social security check to live off, and there we were, two more mouths to feed. She was supposed to get money from the insurance, but the lawyers have been so busy fighting, we haven't seen a dime. Grandma's little check couldn't cover the rent and food too. So, we moved out on the street. Grandma said we had no choice. The City wouldn't help; they said Grandma had to give up custody before they'd help. The City told Grandma she needed help herself, being old and sickly. There was no way they were going to help and let her keep custody. They sent a social services worker to take us away from Grandma, but we hid until the worker left. Once we were on the street, we ate all right at first. That's because Grandma took the money she used to spend on medicine and used it to feed us. We tried a few shelters, but Grandma didn't trust the people at the shelters. She said we were better off on the street than worrying about thieves or drunks or police. She said the people who ran the shelters were in cahoots with the police.

Then Grandma got sick, and things got bad. Once, I brought home some food I stole. Grandma made me take it back to the store and paid for the stolen food out of her next check. Since then, she's been getting worse and worse until now. *Now,* I thought. I couldn't hold back the tears. What were we going to do now? I couldn't get a job: I was only twelve. *I guess I'll have to go back to stealing. If I can take care of us, in two years' time Irene could do a little prostituting. Then, me and Irene won't be a burden to anyone. But Grandma—what about Grandma?* They didn't want to let us in the room. They said we were too young to be in an ICU, whatever that is. Fortunately, the young black nurse (really the receptionist) snuck us back there, supposedly to give information about Grandma's health. Grandma had been in a coma for two days.

"I'm sorry, Grandma. I didn't mean to call the ambulance. You just fell, and I didn't know what else to do." I was crying as I spoke.

"Baby, it's all right."

"And now you're talking about going to Jesus. What are me and Irene supposed to do? You can't leave now! You can't leave!"

"Baby, it's all right. Hush up now. And you take them thoughts of stealing out of your head! Ain't I raised you better than that?"

"Yes, ma'am." Don't ask me how she knew I was thinking about stealing.

"When Jesus comes, He's going to make everything all right."

We'd been on the streets going on two years, and Grandma had been saying the same thing about Jesus all along. *How come Jesus is taking so long?* I thought. *When is he going to get here?*

A doctor came into the room and looked at Grandma's charts. All three of us went as quiet as a mouse. We thought he would say something so that we could know Grandma was coming back. He stood so still as he read. He left the room without a word.

Irene and I kept watching Grandma, and then a nurse came into the room. This one was sort of stout and wore glasses. She was older than the nurse who snuck us into the room and was much sterner in her manner.

"Ma'am," she said.

"Her name is Mrs. Rosa," I blurted out.

The nurse gave me a look. I knew I needed to be quiet, but I felt I had to speak out for Grandma.

"The doctor," she continued, "has advised we need to have the children leave. You're the lady whose family was killed in the bus accident, aren't you?"

"Yes," said Grandma.

"My heart goes out to you. What can I do to help?"

"I'm waiting for Jesus and …" Grandma paused. "I need someone to look after my grandkids."

I was floored. Grandma seemed like she really trusted this lady, and I knew if Grandma could trust her, we could trust her.

"They haven't eaten today."

"Well, Mrs. Rosa, suppose I just take them down to the cafeteria and buy them lunch."

"Thank you," Grandma said. "Now you two go with this nice lady and show some manners."

"But, Grandma, who's going to get you something to eat?" Irene said. "Do you want us to bring you back something?"

Poor Irene. She didn't understand that they feed sick people in hospitals.

"Now, Irene, Grandma's going to be all right."

Irene started to cry.

"I don't want nothing to eat if Jesus is going to come while I'm gone. I want to 'go' with Grandma."

"Baby, it's all right. If Jesus comes while you're eating, I'll ask Him to stay until you come back. And if He can't stay, I'll ask Him to come back while you're here so you won't have to worry about Grandma!"

"Yes, ma'am," she said, and with those words from Grandma, we both followed the nurse as obedient, dutiful children.

As we went by the nurses' station, the young nurse said she'd take us to get something to eat so that the heavier nurse, a supervisor, could handle other patients. When we arrived in the cafeteria, Irene's eyes got as big as silver dollars. The waitress asked us what we wanted to drink. Irene said ginger ale, and I said orange soda, though we both wanted milkshakes. We knew that people really didn't want to spend money on us since we were children living on the street. Sure enough, while we were looking at the menus, the young nurse got a call on her cell phone and left, apologizing, saying she'd be right back. I knew that she wasn't coming back, but I didn't want to let Irene know. They just used the lunch gimmick to get us out of Grandma's room.

Through a serving window that opened to the kitchen, we could see the cook in his white uniform. He smiled as he looked at us, chewing gum rather wildly. He looked directly at me a couple of times, and each time he gave me a wink. I thought the guy was crazy or had a nervous condition. Then he rang the bell in the service window, and a waitress brought over two plates. Each plate had a large cheeseburger with lettuce, tomato, and french fries. When she sat the plates in front of us, she said, "I'll be right back." She returned with two milkshakes, one chocolate (for me) and one vanilla (for Irene).

"How'd you know we wanted milkshakes?" I asked.

"Is that not right?" said the waitress. "That's what Jack said."

"Who's Jack?" I asked.

She pointed to the serving window where I saw the cook, the one who kept laughing and winking at me. Before I could say no, Irene tore into her cheeseburger.

"It's good," she garbled between the gulps of her milkshake and bites of her cheeseburger.

I decided to eat first and get rid of the hyena later.

It's been forty years now, and that hyena is my best friend. Living on the streets, together as partners, we have managed to make it. Sometimes he works as a cook, and sometimes I work construction. Sometimes I panhandle, and sometimes he panhandles. We've slept in alleys, abandoned shacks, lean-to sheds, whatever, to make it through. I've done everything but steal, as I promised Grandma.

After we finished eating, when we came back, Grandma was gone. The nurses looked like they had tears in their eyes when they looked at us.

"Where's Grandma?" I blurted out.

"Well," said the stern nurse, pausing for what seemed a long, long time, "Jesus came."

"Yes," I said, expecting the nurse to go on and tell me the rest of the story.

"Jesus came and took her with Him."

"Yes," I said, still waiting.

"Honey, she's not coming back."

Suddenly it hit me like a ton of bricks.

The stern nurse, Mrs. McCormick, looked at us and said nothing. She didn't know what to say. As I hugged Irene, both of us cried because we couldn't understand how Jesus would break His promise.

The smartest thing I ever did was get Irene off the streets. She wanted to stay with me, but I knew that as a girl she had a much better shot of getting decent foster parents than I did. The stern nurse, Mrs. McCormick, took us both in at first, but I realized she and her husband weren't going to feed us both. I promised Irene when I ran away that I would be by to see her every week, and I did visit. At first, Irene cried and cried, but as I kept my word, she stayed there. It all worked out. The McCormicks even sent Irene to nursing school. They kept telling me they'd take care of me too, but I knew it wouldn't be the same with both of us there. People just don't know how hard it is to get off the street once you're there.

"But Grandma said she'd send Jesus back!"

Irene, at fifty-two, was diagnosed as having a congenital heart defect that placed her in this bed in ICU. *Why her, Lord?* I thought. I had kept my promise to take care of her, and now she was given a death sentence in a couple of hours. "Where's Jesus been all these forty-three years?"

Irene looked directly at Jack, smiled, and closed her eyes, presumably in sleep.

"Jack?" I laughed. Jack was a lot of things, but he wasn't Jesus. I looked at Jack. Suddenly, his demeanor changed. His smile toned down, and he had a look in his eyes that asked *why not*.

Why not? I thought. *Why not? A homeless man, a friend who has been with me all these years?*

"Women," I said laughingly to Jack. "They're so emotional and silly!"

Jack left the room, not in a hurry, as if going to get something from the car. The split second he left, Irene's alarms went off, and the nurses rushed in. Standing outside her room, I kept hearing her say in my head, "Baby, it's all right" In ten minutes, it was over. Irene died. I didn't see Jack again until Irene's burial. I know he saw the questions written on my face. He shook my hand and just sort of walked away.

> Do not be afraid, for I am with you: I will gather your children from the east and gather you from the west. I will say to the north, "Give them up!" and to the south, "Do not hold them back." Bring my sons and daughters from the ends of the earth—everyone who is called by My name, whom I have created for My glory, whom I have formed and made. Isaiah 43:5-7

The Trumpet Shall Sound!

We all saw it. That's the problem! I was recalled from my vacation in Newington when the first sighting was made. Such a phenomenon had disturbed the best minds, for its occurrence was so sudden and flabbergasting. Data from the farthest flung of our satellites had not increased our understanding of its nature.

The Big Bangers interpreted its appearance as confirmation that their explanation of the universe had been right. This appearance, they said, had begun its travel at the origin of the universe. Within the phenomenon, they said, lay the transformation of all order to the next level. Of course, the Bangers did not offer an identification of the next step but merely posited such a step should exist. No doubt, their logic projecting a next step grew from human hunger to have a mental outcome the present mind has not grasped. Men need to feel needed. Another step would need interpreters and guides, visionaries armed with the scientific and mathematical tools that could reduce a previously unknown experience to the language lesser minds could ideate.

Throughout the world, every conceivable and readily available scientific instrument was trained to provide insight into the phenomenon. It never occurred to us, the intelligentsia, to view the phenomenon as anything other than a happening.

What I saw was an overwhelming, amorphous, non-translucent, non-transparent presence, a presence that totally consumed the sky. On the outer perimeter of the presence were hazel fringes that resembled aurora borealis on a miniature, almost dismissive scale. In computer terms, the presence seemed a desktop screen on which all the celestial bodies that had been observed before the appearance of the phenomenon took their place. Those celestial bodies continued their functions and trajectories, as if unaffected by the arrival. In fact, none of the observable astronomical relationships that pre-dated the phenomenon's appearance changed in any manner. Not even radio astronomy recorded any changes that were attributable to the phenomenon's presence.

Yet, the phenomenon's sudden appearance was incredibly unnerving. It could be seen day or night. Its distance from Earth derived from mathematical computations of known celestial bodies seemed so enormous it was frightening. Imagine a cloud so large it filled the entire sky on one side of the Earth's hemisphere. Now factor into your distance equation the best scientific instruments you can access pointing in a rock-solid manner to a conclusion that the cloud's distance from Earth exceeds one million centillion light years! Would you not fear, if such a cloud was travelling toward you so rapidly, defining a speed you could not imagine? After all, we figured it had to be traveling at some incredible speed to appear from nowhere as it did. Its presence moved the original Big Bang point a lot further back in time than we had ever imagined. More important than revising the origin point of the universe was the fear that a phenomenon traveling so fast included such powerful natural forces as to render Earth helpless, at the mercy of its caprice.

Flabbergasting to all scientific minds were continuing reports sighting the phenomenon's visibility at the same time over the entire Earth. The experience of universal simultaneous observation fascinated and panicked at the same time. The earth being a globe, universal simultaneous observation evidenced an existence in a fourth dimension no one understood. The problem with attributing the universal observations to mass hallucination is that in the hallucination scenario, you cannot rely on scientific instruments or the scientific method, since the reasoning mind cannot approach data objectively. In universal mass hallucination, how does one know when one is hallucinating and when one is not?

Still, there were a lot of outspoken thinkers who argued that mass hallucination was the phenomenon's explanation. It was indeed true that none of the instruments known to man had provided any direct endemic data of the phenomenon. It was as if the phenomenon did not exist apart from observation by the human eye. Spectral analysis of the phenomenon did not yield any data. Photographs of the phenomenon did not evidence its presence. Still, the same measuring instruments were providing usable data in other scientific experiments that had no relation to the phenomenon. If humans were hallucinating, what caused the hallucination? Could we be the target of an alien intelligence whose scientific superiority was evident in their ability to project such a universal hallucination? Were we ignoring the signs of an impending peril we could deflect, mute, or minimize before Earth was damaged?

Most minds shrank from the hallucination scenario, frightened by the negative and defeatist conclusions that adoption of that approach ultimately derived. Sending aloft probe after probe, humanity united in what we saw as the biggest challenge to our existence. Even though no menacing activity had been observed that had its origin in the phenomenon, we struggled as one to avoid a negative outcome of a happening we did not understand.

The clock struck midnight Greenwich Mean Time May 31. I cast a harmless glance out of my window at the clear evening sky. For us East Coast types, an American spring cheered the mood, escaping the drudgery of continual investigation of what seemed an adamantine riddle. Six long months of mental assault by the brightest minds on the planet had not advanced our understanding of the phenomenon. We were stuck, depressed, and at our wit's ends, constantly applying the acumen of human knowledge to a problem that would not yield the solution we expected, namely an answer to the riddle.

Then it happened! At midnight Greenwich Mean Time, I say! When it happened, we knew that neither science nor politics mattered. When we saw it, we knew perfectly that it was not a hallucination. In one moment, humanity stood awed by an unexpected insight into the phenomenon.

It was a simple motion, a very simple motion. The entire world saw a single eyelid and a single eyebrow as the eye blinked a blink that covered the entire phenomenon. The phenomenon we had been observing before the blink was the pupil of an eye that had not moved. So now we belong to the ages, the voices that did not use our hearts when we heard the trumpets call. They did call, and we muted their voices, not expecting this moment to arrive.

> But let me tell you a wonderful secret God has revealed to us. Not all of us will die, but we will all be transformed. It will happen in a moment, in the blinking of an eye, when the last trumpet is blown. For when the trumpet sounds, the Christians who have died will be raised with transformed bodies. And then we who are living will be transformed so that we will never die. For our perishable earthly bodies must be transformed into heavenly bodies that will never die. 1 Corinthians 15:51-53

Printed in the United States
By Bookmasters